CUM & COFFEE

Poetry & Pros

WOLFE PARNELL

Copyright 2023 Travis R. Parnell
All rights reserved. No part of this book may be reproduced in any form or by any electronic means- except in he case of brief quotations embodied in articles and reviews- without the written permission of the publisher.

INTRODUCTION

Beautiful, alluring, & sensual poems celebrating love, intimacy, and HER overall sensual indulgence. These poems are slow-motion tongue verbs that glide inside her white waters; full, plump, coco-lip nouns that soft suck on her sensuality; hard, thick, long stanzas that fill you; and strong waistline-rotation verses that hold you still. These poems are your mind-gasms, so enjoy, my loves

BOOK 1

BODY & MIND

HIGHLY MELANATED

Scrumptious chocolate lips,
Golden mahogany skin,
Sparkling almond eyes
She's a Black Woman,
A highly melanated superwoman,
With her ancient melanin being the source of her powers
Her soulful eyes gaze into my pineal gland,
Such sapiosexual seductive allure
Delicious, thick lips of African coco-brown sugar,
And divine lips of ebony, honey-dipped yoni goodness,
I wish to kiss both,
Tasting her essence
Mmmhh....
It's shea butter, coconut oil, jasmine essence with a hint of pineapple and mango
Lord, forgive me, for I wish to be baptized in the wetness of her intellect,
Sliding deep inside her chakras
I wish to strip her of her past hurts,
Not so I can have her naked,
But so I can bathe her in my words,
Apply the coconut oil of my intentions,
And adorn her with my actions
Her figure is pyramid architectural design,
A true, ancient wonder of this world
She makes my mind erect,
Causing my body to think

POET

Excuse me, Miss,
I am sure you're not looking for some all-thumbs, self-centered, pretty boy,
I'm sure you're looking for a man to drip a cocktail of words and hot breath into your ear,
Lips brushing against your lobes,
Jangling your precious pearls
You're looking for a Poet, my love,
With verses moving just as suggestively as his hands,
Full of double entendres,
And equally setting fire to your imagination,
Transforming your once innocent swaths of skin into tiny flames,
Flickering erotic signals to your brain that you always thought were reserved for more intimate locations
He'll write you a bottle of red wine,
Whisper it into your veins,
Transforming your body into a tsunami of elevated sensations,
Everlasting pleasure rippling along your surface
You deserve a Poet, my love
You deserve some aural sex.

FINGERS

My words caress you,
Paint images between your thighs,
Imagination unfolds,
Blooms,
As do your woman petals
Sitting on your bed,
Legs open,
You are a book, between your thighs are pages,
My words written in your mind,
And now on the lines of your wetness
You touch yourself,
Longing to have me perform poetry,
Reciting my words on your clitoris
Your fingers scribbling,
Performing calligraphy across your parting lips
You moan... soft... deep
Verbalize my words in gasps,
Express in articulate vowels
Wetness utters your pleasure
Fingers slide slowly
Deep... Your waters speak sloppy audio,
Slender fingers dance,
Moving with boldness,
Determination,
Frantic focus,
Causing you to inhale,
Immersed in soft folds,
Sink into your ocean,
Submerged in waves,
Evoking rippling pleasure

White cream swirls
You clench, squeeze
Moaning profanity
Your rose bud smiles,
You laugh with delight, overcome by tingles,
Joyfully filled with shudders
You can feel my words,
They stroke your precious walls,
Pressed against your g-spot
Moving with firm, yet delicate pressure
Filling you... wetness... creaminess
They are he applause,
An accolade of your rupture
Your fingers coated in your praise

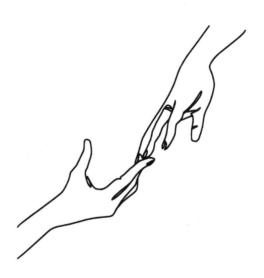

LATE NIGHT CONVOS

Your lips and I conversed last night,
We tickled each other's aural senses with feather-tongued strokes,
They whispered their deep, moist secrets to me
The ears of my tongue soaked in their hidden words,
As I inhaled honey-sweet breath on my lips
Their dialogue was candy-floss sweetness,
Light, sticky dialect of deep, dark, hidden thoughts
My tongue floated like mist,
Wandering about through the labyrinth of your mind
Silent... almost invisible
Only they could see the faint whisper of my mouth's openness,
And as gently as morning dew, they confessed their deepest desires,
Glossing my lips.... my mind
They introduced me to your encompassing legs, and their grip felt like a summer breeze tone,
Warm... light... faint... cooling
And your body replied in a 10.0 magnitude of throbbing,
Her words were full and swollen with articulate shakes,
And my mouth was silently tentative,
Absorbing all your body had to say,
Made mental notes on the paper of my taste buds
And tonight...
Tonight, we are going to converse some more....
But this time, I have free nights

LET'S TALK

We masturbate,
Playing with each other's minds
Fondling it... groping it
Stimulating the motions of 'mind-blowing' sex
Your clouded, sensual mind condenses,
A downpour of heavenly, but devilish thoughts
Causing the hardness of my focus to pulse
Tease each other with whispered promises of possibilities
Slowly pull each other to the brink of ejaculating new thinking
But pause... Stop
We prolong the moment
Titillating, we tickle each other's want,
Seducing it with nimble fingers,
Offer playful hints with long gazes
Nibble on the bottom lip of anticipation
Lick the lips of patience,
Slowly undressing our longing
Revealing butt-naked intentions
Yet, we don't stop
No need to race to the finish line of our mental release
Yet, we sink beneath the surface,
Becoming lost in the under-currant of passion
Hold our breath,
Tiny bubbles of fading restraint float to the surface
Pop... We watch them
Yet, we dive deeper into the abyss of lust
10,000 leagues into the sea of desire
Discover the lost city of this erotic Atlantis
This is what we do when we... Talk

NIBBLE

Your lips, I just wish to nibble on,
My tongue dipping between the silk-like folds of your lips
Every taste bud pressed,
Every crevice filled
I just love when your love begins to spill,
Dark chocolate melanin wrapped in my Hershey-like kisses
Skin molded on top of skin
Deep passions filling the air again
Stagnant moans begin to take control
You see, my Queen
Your lips, I just want to nibble on,
Allow my teeth to sink in,
Getting a taste of how much you've missed your King
Joints pressing on top of me
Hershey kisses from your elbow to your feet
Melanin skin fused as we become one
Our world colliding,
A true clash of titanic pleasure
I just want to nibble on it, my love
Stagnant moans suffocating conversation
I need your sweet vibrations,
Organic temptation,
Deadly sensations
I just want to nibble on it

ROOM SERVICE

"You will never truly have me,"
She thought to herself, as he kissed her lips with the deepest of passion
Her eyes screamed,
"I will probably only disappoint you."
Both continued to play out a charade as it unraveled on the bedspread,
Imitating a love neither was ready to give
"I will never give you all of me,"
She thought while he rubbed her thighs and wrapped her beautiful limbs around his
"I don't want to play this game anymore,"
She whispered as he pressed her head back against the bed frame, pushing in deep
She gasped...
Her body became paralyzed as his strokes became a little more aggressive
"This isn't right,"
She told him, digging her ¼ inch nails into his caramelized skin
She pressed deeper, as he watched her body contort into figures neither was prepared for
Her mind raced as his tongue sunk between her silk-like folds,
Sucking her nectar,
Sending chills down her now arched spine
He came up for air, placing his face against her neck,
Pulling her body closer to his, filling the space between the sheets
She lay there, watching his devilish, passionate eyes close

She knew he had to go home...
A home far from her own
"She will never love you the way I do,"
She snickered as she inhaled the sweet herb tingling her lips
"Relax...,"
She said to herself, inhaling deeper now
Tears of sensual confusion streamed down her face
She knew all he will ever get from her was a taste...
Their hearts will always be in two different places while thy filled these sheets and empty spaces
After all, they both knew that what they have isn't more than a little...
Room service

FULL MOON

I wish to love you like the full moon
With silent grace,
Offer you majestic presence,
Show you 360 degrees of full circular pleasure
Love you with beauty,
Regal. Silent
I wish to control your spasms as the moon controls the oceans
Affect the tides of your rushing waters
Move your waters
Eclipse shadows of past hurts,
Past monotonous sex lives
Bring forth new beginnings through my poetic light
I wish to orbit the planet of you,
Your oceans and your lands
Use the gravitational pull of my mouth to make you spin,
Leave you like its atmosphere- breathless
Drive you crazy- lunar-tic
Touch your femininity,
Have you floating,
Suspended in the black, velvet skies of our room
I wish to love you like the full moon, my love,
And control your earthly waters

DANCE

I'll leave you with these tiny strings of letters,
Sliding their little feet and curves through the motions of a tango,
That perfect dance that's so much more than lead and follow
It's where the arch of your back begins,
Just a hint, a dip
It's where the sensual warmth first begins to spread,
As I move you without a single kiss,
Without the pawing of adolescent passion,
Or the hurry of men who think women are merely tools for masturbation
This is where- fully dressed- our steps become sentences,
Our dance becomes play, then passion, then foreplay
Here is where dance becomes gravity,
Desire magnetic,
Two bodies first circling,
Then coming together, until, the night at its peak, clothes fall away
Slowly, no rush,
Your lingerie long ago soaked through and pointless
Here is the place I lay you down,
Where a poem becomes that dance,
And this time, as we come together,
We cum... together
Waking up to hold you,
Just these sleepy minutes of peace with you wrapped in my arms,
And yours holding mine,

As if you have now found a place to belong here against me,
And never wanting to leave,
And in spite of our stubborn alarm and its insistence,
It is time for other things, my love,
And this is heaven enough for me

NAKED

If I decided to manumit your mind before touching the gentle flow between your thighs,
Would you still think I want you?
You see, I'm not one to chase after big assess and perked-up breasts,
I'm trying to dive into your intellectual side,
Undressing your mind,
Exposing your doubts, insecurities, and things you've wept to
Give it to me so deep and pure, that even the sheets are soaked with knowledge
Conversations about love, sex, and passion are never clouded
Tranquil off foreplay that lasts for hours
Our words creating beautiful collages
What I need from you could never be achieved in just this physical form
I would rather unlock your thoughts,
Before unlocking your thighs
My mind exploring the sacred temple that lies beneath your clothing
I need to know, my love,
Can you get naked for me with your temple still covered?
Imagine our love being like that,
Mental stimulation leading to sensual perspiration
This connection is undeniable,
Impossible to fake
All I want to do is to get you…
Naked

HER CONFESSIONS

She whispered in my ear,
Her deepest confessions
She wants me to put her in her glorious position,
Face down... ass up... back arched
Said she wants to be biting in the pillow,
Screaming into it
Hearing her muffled moans,
As my hardness slides deep and long into her softness
Wants to feel my sharp, stinging hands punish her ass with each thrust
Wants to feel her blood rushing to her head,
Scattered inside her,
Fountains up to her throbbing clit
Making it hard... zapped with the electrical volts of my cock
She wants her ass cheeks to burn,
Giving her a delicious sting of pins and needles
She wants to feel empowered,
By being submissive,
Being held down under my forceful thrusts
She wants to be my Queen,
By being my slave,
Made to submit to my relentless shaft of Kings
Made to accept strong forces of reprimanding hands
She likes how it's raw... instinctive... carnal... savage
Yet, make her feel human,
Make her feel like a woman
The precision makes her dance,
The rhythmic beat of bodies clapping,

An applaud to this beautiful performance
She wants an encore
She wants me deep... deeper... deeper
Hard, long strokes that touch her roof,
Giving her that bittersweet pain deep inside her stomach
She wants to become drunk off my intoxicating 'cock-tail'
Feel lightheaded... giddy upon release
Her true confession...
She wants me to put her in her glorious position...
Face down... ass up... back arched

CONTROL

You lay flat
Mouth opened,
Eyes closed,
Back arched
Volcanic clouds of coarse moans erupting skywards
Dark ashes of sudden, pending release fill the room
Lust... need
Pleasure implodes in your stomach,
Eruption imminent
You plead... request,
Beg for me to release your body from the stronghold of my magical touches
My fingers titillating your flawless skin,
Pressing against your melanin
You freeze...
Dumbstruck by your own shudders
Arms wrapped tightly around me,
Creating ragged, passionate work communicative art along my body,
Your body is art,
Mahogany carved melanin sculpture
My nails pushing onto your delicate pores,
Push, yet hold you,
Imprisoning you in your own bodily spasms
You plead again...
Confused audible expressions escaping your mouth
Stomach tightening,
Heart racing...
You beg for release

I stop...
Declining your request
You scream.... Shhhh
Remember, I control your temple

THAT MOMENT

When I first merged your lips with mine, that moment...
That instance of body-tingling, tongue penetration,
It was a beautiful contradiction
A clash... a clash of titans
A massive collision of slow-eased release,
And sharp, sudden burst of emotions... of pleasure
A clattering of tingles,
While still soothing our raging wants...
Our deepest needs
It was a thunderstorm of desire,
Before the lightening of electrical lust,
Followed by a rainbow of delight,
The radiant spectrum of pleasures
Finding the liquid gold of your sweet woman nectar at the end of our lust-filled thunderstorm
It was loud,
Yet, it was silent,
An explosion of fulfilled anticipation
The deafening-silence of stillness
It was harmony, A low song
Soft... slow... seductive
But a carnival,
Frenzied... exciting... decadent
It was urgent and immediate,
Yet, unhurried and considered
That moment... that instance
When I first kissed you,
It was a beautiful contradiction,
Of how our worlds collided... and became one

OWNERSHIP

Say it...
Say it with vexed surrender
Gasp...
Fill your lungs until they swell,
Then let the words grate against your vocal cords as you proclaim your submission
Say it...
Say it as your breath stammers
Falters... fumbles in your mouth
Declare it... affirm your yielding to my authority
Say it with passionate profanity
Plead to the almighty
Grit your teeth,
Crushing your determination in your jaws
Say it...
Snarl your succumbing to my prevailing title
Apologize... plead
Implore me to govern you as you offer yourself
Look into my gaze
Say it with whimpered softness
Kneel before me with your eyes,
Ask for permission with your pupils
Bite your bottom lip as you mumble these words
Say it...
Release coarse squeals as you exhale
Let your vulnerability pull these words from your belly,
As you articulate in graining expression acquiesce to my proprietorship
Say it with the H2o audio of your eloquent dialogue

Say it... say it again... and again... again!
Repeat it like an echo
Tell me...
Who owns your pussy

SUCKER

I am a sucker, my love
For your dark chocolate-dipped thighs, and your golden honey-dew lips
Oh my, those lips...
Creating that banana-shaped smile, and that strawberry-flavoured kiss
Staring into those almond-shaped eyes, holding those butterscotch hips,
I just want to make love to you,
Encompassing you in my arms, basking in this titillating bliss
I'm a sucker for your smooth coconut skin and the smell of your natural black woman hair,
Oh, what an aphrodisiac your moisturizer and herbs release into the air
I'm a sucker for your skin, and how suggestively your hands move,
Digging deep into my flesh... oh, what sweet, sensual battle wounds
I'm a sucker for your verbs, your pronouns, your adjectives, and more,
Your thoughts, your intellect, oh, what sapiosexual seductive allure
I'm a sucker for your laugh, your voice, and just your overall passion,
Your corny jokes, your choices, and oh my, your sexy bodily action
I'm a sucker for your love, your moans, and our silent moments,

Your past, your fears, and oh, what hidden components
I value what you say, my love, and I admire all that you do,
Basically, what I'm saying...
I'm simply a sucker...
A sucker for you

BURNING CREATION

He was like a candle,
An elegant, evocative flame,
A smooth, sturdy, provocative frame
He would burn himself,
And smile while he melts,
To keep her warm amongst the coldness,
And give her light amidst the darkness
From his own sweat,
He held himself down
He might have flickered, once in a while,
As he tussled with the winds,
But he would never be blown out
For her,
He would burn and burn and burn
While there she sat,
His favourite poem,
Waiting seductively
For him to be enslaved by her every dirty word,
While his flame engulfed every inch of her,
Burning her with magic,
With passion,
A kiss mimicking the supernova
A kiss so explosive,
It created another galaxy within their universe

SAPIOSEXUAL LOVE

Your mind is beautiful
It arouses me,
Makes my intellect get a hard-on
Makes my curiosity pulse
Makes me want to slide deep and long into the wetness of your wisdom
I want to taste your imagination,
Soft suck on your ambition,
Give back-shots to your motivation
And I love... oh I so love,
When your compassion kisses my faith,
When your values saddle my morals and ride me
I love when you use the mouth of your heritage and take the hardness of my dark, hard past and deep-throat it
I love how you make my mind cum,
Making me orgasm new thinking
Your beautiful mind does things to me your body could never do

STOLEN

I will take your strength without permission,
Leaving you limp like cooked spaghetti
Steal your focus,
Slip it out of your pocket of concentration
Swipe your coordination,
Snatch it away from your grip of synchronized motion
Claim ownership of your breath,
Leaving you gasping for air
Feel it slip through the fingers of your lungs
Confiscate your vision
Abduct your sight,
Leave you with a haze with your 20-20 clarity blurred
Pillage your restraint,
Take it by force from the strong hold of your limits
Ransack your vocal cords
Misappropriate your moans,
Leaving your mouth hallow and only be able to scream silently
Embezzle your senses
Siphon off wetness,
Drawing it from deep inside you
Funnel it via your clit and place it in the container of my mouth
Defraud you of your release
Kidnap your orgasm,
Hold it for ransom
I will leave you a victim of my bedroom robbery

SECRET WATERS

80% of the body is water,
And between the mountains of your thighs is the source
of your bodily waters,
Mother Nature's fountain of youth
My mouth,
Warm. Moist, but dry,
Ready to suck
Longing for the oceans between your thighs to be
explored by me,
For the waves of your yoni to ripple over my tongue
I lick my lips,
Tongue dives,
Sinks into the silent rapids of your trenches
Your ocean,
Salty, but sweet,
Nourishing
Rides the crest of your vulva waves
Swims deep into the swirls between your folds
Guarding a deep secret
I inhale deep,
Holding my breath
Dive in search of your soft pearl,
Hidden in the core of your thighs,
Only to be discovered by an experienced seaman
My mouth ebbs and flows with the tide of your moans
Washed afresh,
Drifting on the sea of our sex

MOTHER NATURE

I want to suck you like lightening,
Fuck you like thunder
Have my tongue create static electricity coursing through the nerve endings of your yoni
Causing your body to judder and jolt,
Exploding into Mother Nature's creamy downpour
Washing my tongue with the white waters of your fountain of youth
Sparks of buzz in your curled toes
High voltage of tongue-powered tingles strike the peak of your clitoris and zaps your body into full submission
I want to fuck you like thunder
Deep... hard... sudden... booming
Nonsensical screams of pleasure grate against your vocal cords
Thunderous thrusts causing moans to rumble from the pit of your stomach and boom out of your mouth
My thrusts digging into your epicenter causing you to vibrate... tremble,
Your legs rumbling with pleasure
Fuck you with hard decibels of penetrations that cause you to reverberate
Have your sounds fill the sky of our room as your orgasms precipitate onto the landscape of our bed
Showering me
I want to suck you like lightening,
Fuck you like thunder

GPS

Your moans are my GPS
They are my guide so I don't lose my sense of direction over your mesmerizing contours
They soothe my frantic moments while I travel along the historic architectural wonders of your body
They guide my tongue to the location of your pleasures,
My audio-navigation
You moan
My tongue heads toward the destination of your slow-eased release
I become lost,
Become dizzy with disorientation inside your mountainous walls,
Wandering aimlessly
Your moans grate against your vocal cords
I retrace my tongue's steps through the folds of your yoni
I've found you
Take a left at the roundabout of your nib
Take the first exit
I head towards your entrance
Your long moans are organic fuel to my engine,
Giving me power
I speed along your drenched motorway
Traveling up your alley towards your g-spot
Accelerate
Race pass the legal speed limit
Speed cameras of your walls flash,
Triggered by my lightening pace,

Trying to capture the moment
The police of your logic pursue me
I press my tongue down on the throttle of your nib,
Your engine revs loud
The wheels of your eyes spin,
Burning images on the tarmac of your eyelids
Your neck jerks back from the g-force speed of my tongue
The fuel of your desire burns fast
Traveling with ferocious velocity
Speed... race
Grip the steering wheel of my head
Brace yourself
Wrap the seatbelt of your legs around my neck,
Try to slam on the brake release
Screech loudly as you reach your final destination
Aaaahhhhh...

CHERISHED

My woman...
With my words, I wish to be granted full access to your secret place,
A place where the sun envies our brightness,
And the soft breeze whispers our love in faint fragrance of baby's breath and jasmine
In here, I wish to have full passage to your beautiful gardens,
A table spread in our honor;
Adorned with your succulent fruits that drip with the sweet nectar of your goodness
I wish to feast, my love,
And be exhilarated in your love
In this place, we shall not fear to lose ourselves in each other,
For these gates have no need for a keeper,
For I alone possess the ancient key
In this place, time has no restraints,
So I happily take the lead
Gently... softly
From the lofty heights of this place, we shall broadcast our undying devotion for one another,
So that it echoes throughout the heavens
And who is that one to dare presume it possible to unravel the ties that bind our souls in a perpetual state of oneness?
For there is greater hope of the sun freeing the planets from its embrace, or the stars refusing to light the universe with their celestial glow, than of out union dissolving into obscurity
My love, take solace in knowing that you are most cherished

HYPNOTIC

I haven't forgotten, my love,
The snowflakes laced across your broad hips,
Melted by the gushing white rivers that ran from within,
'till the cloth between us may as well have been skin
I haven't forgotten,
The candy cane shells and the beautiful valley between them,
As you were winter shades and island skin above me
I haven't forgotten,
What it meant to abandon the world,
And all its complications that night,
To rise and fall together,
To press my fingers into the epicenters of your bodily quakes,
And feel your tsunamis crash against the shores of my palms
You were the inspiration for my finest poetry,
A collaboration written in the dark
There, your body spoke a language all its own
The breathless cries which escaped your lips could never have been captured or contained on paper,
But they were written deep within my heart
I haven't forgotten, my love,
What it meant to touch you,
And I haven't forgotten,
What it means to love you
A true hypnotic memory

ALLURED CONFUSION

She stared at me,
With her stunning green eyes,
Which were clearly, just a second ago, overwhelmed with tears,
Tears of confusion,
Of disbelief,
Yet complete understanding
She stared at me,
In both awe and fear,
As if she wasn't sure,
If she wanted my next words to be filled with
unconditional truth or utter lies with immense allure,
For she must have finally known that I have another,
A life partner, a wife
But she still asked anyway,
"Do you love me?"
With all the strength her defeated heart could muster
Yes would certainly be the truth
No would be an uncertain, yet "right" answer
A white lie, a valiant act,
That would ultimately save us both the pain and agony
we would have to endure apart, right?
I wondered, but couldn't speak
We stared in awkward silence,
For a moment that felt like eons,
But she was relentless,
Leaning in to kiss me,

And for the life of me,
I couldn't stop her,
And right there and then, she had her answer
And for the life of her,
She kissed me deeper,
And she knew she had me

WRITE A POEM

Are you a Poet, Mr. Parnell?
Yes, my love
Now allow me to use my fingers to write a poem along your body,
Unlocking the gates of your restraint
Punctuation of swift, darting fingertip movements,
Transcribing your high-pitched, nonsensical screams of pleasure
Dot the "Is" of intimate imagination,
Cross the "Ts" of your bodily tingles
Calligraphy strokes,
Elegant. Gentle
Create images. Masterpieces
Mona Lisa-like fame painted on your one-of-a-kind bodily canvas
The art of finger-brush strokes that create words,
Write a sonnet along your melanin tapestry that would inspire Solomon and Shakespeare
Slip and sink between the pages of your woman valley
I would like to hike and scale the mountainous walls of your mind
Write late at nights,
In the mornings,
At lunch time
Short interludes,
Full epic chronicles,
From my sensual words that ignite your bodily flames
Trace geometric shapes,

Focused, sudden strokes from a haiku of pleasure
Smooth out and unfold the soft, crumpled pages of your lips
Reignite the flames of your sex life
Script pros on them,
Write a chapter around your contours,
Pressing the pen of my piercing fingertips beneath you,
And create a novel along the archaeological masterpiece of your walls,
Until you release a Pulitzer Prize mind-orgasm

HOLY SURRENDER

I am your master
Submissive is your position,
Prayer-like
You worship my length
Face down… ass up
Offer yourself to me,
Your body… your moans… your wetness
Hail me,
Proclaim aloud your pending arrival
Grip the bed sheets
Don't touch me, peasant!
Body tambourine shakes,
Choir of tingles announces the coming of your precious orgasm
I own it…
I enter your wet sanctuary,
Baptizing my girth in your precious waters,
My fountain of youth
You surrender to my thrusting sermon
Place my hands on the base of your spine,
Holding you down
You catch the erotic spirit,
Rejoice, and call my name
I hit the roof of your heavenly bud,
You see angels
Holding you hostage
You are my slave,
Deep inside your own body

BEDROOM BULLY

I am your authority
Your Sir. Your master
I will use my hardness to make you yield
Part the waters of your resistance with my rod of power
Assault you with strong strokes
Intimidate you with my girth
Threaten you with stamina
Become your mattress predator,
Mother Nature's intent
Attack you with vicious force
Punish your beauty with dangerous levels of deep thrusts
Strip you of all feminist power
Make you surrender,
Submit
Bow down to my erect domination
Take away your resolve
Make you pay with your moans
Tax you of your orgasms
I own it...
Rob you of your inhibitions
Make you feel my wrath
Attack you with lustful vengeance
Take ownership of your throbbing
Snatch away your tingles
Make you pledge your wetness to my possession
Control your shudders
Punish you with deep thrusts

Make you feel my want
Terrorize your orgasms
I am your authority
I am your bedroom bully

MORE THAN...

I don't wish for you to only cum,
I want you to sing
Let the octaves rise up out of your mouth
Create a melody, and perform an ode to your release
Harmonize with the song of your nerve endings
Hum a tune of yours,
And set free the choir of pleasures encased in your vocal cords
I don't wish for you to only cum,
I want you to meditate,
Mumble a mantra
Align your chakras,
And ascend, going beyond yourself,
Discovering who you are
Become alien to your own self
Tune in to the frequency of this universe
Become calm,
Still
Hear the whisper of butterfly wings
I don't wish for you to only cum,
I want you to speak a new language
Converse with ancestors
Translate the scripts of ancient Egyptians
Chant a spiritual dialect
Punctuate your sentences with profanity
Speak in phonics,
Expressing your thoughts in vowel sounds
I don't wish for you to only cum,

I want you to speak with the creator
Call out His name,
Praise Him,
Become touched by the Holy Spirit
Testify,
Speak a sermon of thanks
I don't wish for you to only cum,
I want you to feel weak,
Spent
Feel your limbs become heavy with scrumptious fatigue
Your muscles to become exhausted,
For your body to melt,
Weighted with bliss,
Light with release
For it to feel renewed,
Feel depleted
I don't wish for you to only cum...
I want you to feel more... much more

DRUNKEN LOVE

I'm so drunk off the love I have for you
Sometimes I wish I could go back in time with you,
Just to relive our first kiss over and over again
That instance of body-tingling penetration of my tongue between your lips
Body to body
Lost in the lustful conversations of our love
Sometimes, I wish I could go back to the moment I first made you smile,
Those chocolate-honey lips
Those sparkling, almond-shaped eyes
I'm captivated by your voice, your scent, and how easily our conversations piled
Lost in your touch and the beautiful shape of you for hours
Sometimes, I wish I could go back to the moment I first felt your honey-dew drip,
Coating the atmosphere with the steam of your wonders
I was swallowed whole by your majestic presence and touch
To be held by you until the sun came up
I made mistakes, causing our waves to get rough,
But you remained patient with me, and my jagged thoughts of love
My heart still races for you,
Waking up to the sight of you every morning
It's like waking up to you for the first time each time

Moist hands, thoughts racing, and shortness of breath
Sometimes, I wish I knew when you first undressed my mind
When the first "I love you" that you said tickled every bone in my body
I'm so drunk off the love I have for you,
Since the first moment you made me cum deep beyond physical penetration
Those moments where our syllables and nouns made love in every conversation
Thank you, my love

TONGUEOLOGY

I want to...
Use my tongue to paint images of pleasure on your clitoris,
Creating a masterpiece of delight on your yoni
Swift tongue-brush strokes that colour your senses
Develop a spectrum of vivid tingles coursing through your body
My tongue masterfully drawing out your pink pearl,
Making your body silently scream,
Their sounds echo in the arch of your back
Hum inside you,
Pulsate in your walls,
Create a rhythmic beat in the delicate softness of your rose bud
Moan semiotics of pleasure
Express your desires in strong punctuation of clenched fists
Phonics of curled toes,
Eloquence of flared fingers opened wide,
Kinesics bubbling urgency
Your insides becoming tense
Linguistics of your walls clenching,
Translated in the throbbing of 8,000 nerve endings
Stretched vocabulary convulsions
Syntax of your body's language
This is the way of my Tongueology

WHAT I WANT...

I want to suck on you,
My tongue imbibing the sweet, thick sap of your woman flower,
Drink from your nature's fountain,
Have your inner thighs wrapped around my head like headphones,
Breathing in your sweet aroma
Listen to the ocean of your yoni's pleasure washing along the banks of your meaty jaws
Gloss my tongue with your tidal waves of pure pleasure
Engulf your rose bud with my warm mouth and sing it a lullaby
Create crackles of electricity through the tip of your clit,
Your body jolting as showers of rain flow from your swollen yoni,
Mother Nature's showers
Finding the pot of gold at the rainbow's end of your arched back,
Bringing broad sets of smiles to both lips
Allowing your stream of liquid gold to run down my chin
Captain my tongue to circumnavigate your vast ocean
Let me explore the undiscovered depths of your ocean floor,
Descend
Pressure of your clenched muscles griping my tongue the deeper I go

Lick you long
Stroke your wetness with unhurried desire
Gentle pull... teasing you,
Drawing spherical rings around your bud
Rotate...
Tongue-orbiting the sun of your woman button
Exploring the galaxy of your need
Now, my love, may I suck on you?

TIGHTER

"Tighter!"
She said as my fingertips began to grip tighter against her smooth flesh,
Beads of sweat forming at the top of my chest,
Dripping onto the bedspread,
Soaked with perspiration
Her hands started to tear from the base of my wrists
Her body choking for air, as her fists pushed deep into the mattress
Legs dangling in distress
Her walls contracting
Slowly... our minds collapsing
Releasing my grip, only to taste her honey-sweet breath,
Piercing the barrier of what was once her innocence
I pledged my allegiance on her sacred temple's steps
Her deepest thoughts etched into my back,
Our own passionate battlefield
I was hers. She was mine
My constitution tattooed with the flick of my lips
My tongue... in so deep between her crumbling walls
Tranquility was found,
After passionate chaos was made
"Tighter!"
She said as she choked for enjoyment
Her body becoming numb
Blood rushing to her head with each squeeze
With each thrust

Leaving battle wounds etched onto my shoulder blades,
On the sheets,
As she whispered,
"Tighter..."

MY QUEEN

My Queen,
May every morning be like this?
Subtle heartbeats against melanin skin
Fingernails etched into my back,
Revealing your most sensual of secrets
Soft kisses exchanged under lavender scents
May every morning be like this?
Greeted by the golden rays of the sun,
And the fresh, misty dew winds,
Melanin rays of your smile,
With fingertips travelling along my vertebrae,
Legs spread on top of feather-filled blankets
May every morning be like this?
Hips touching the small marks of passion on my body,
Teeth marks embedded into my ribcage,
Thoughts of loving you until my dying days
May every morning be like this?
Confessions of my love spilling from my lips,
As your pineapple juice drips from my fingertips
Everything you are is everything in me
May every morning be like this?

LOVE

When I think of you,
I realize how long I've been without your touch
Your long nails etching your sensual thoughts into my back,
Always so artistic
Days and weeks starting to feel like months and years
These are the moments I miss,
Staring into your soulful eyes,
Your legs wrapped around my waist,
My cold hands pressed against the warmth of your skin
Premature "I love you's" filling our room,
As your kisses leave my thoughts completely tongue-tied
I'm in awe at how we make every night feel like paradise
Our eyes locked,
Minds hazy,
Passion rough,
Spasms heavy
We're lost in a world full of gushing rivers and sensual battle wounds
I cannot begin to tell you what goes through my mind when our souls are climaxing
I get so tipsy off our mental stimulation
Elated from your cum-stained, nonsensical abbreviations
Weakness from constant meat-to-meat penetration
Sigh...
These days and weeks are starting to feel like months and years
I will never get enough of your warm, sensual love

CLARITY

When we make love,
The phrase becomes ambiguous,
Stripped of intelligence
It becomes raw... unrefined
We are filled with disorder
Tranquil and stillness erased
Our ripples become tsunamis
Rationality crumbles
Our wisdom become bewildered
Clarity clouds over to become gray skies of vagueness
Our minds become chaotic,
Frantic with want... desire... need
Insight becomes visually impaired,
Blindness by haziness
Where are we?
We are in our own land of "wood and water"
Knocked unconscious by Jamaican mystification
Composed logic is torn apart by confused, lustful fury
Thoughts are shattered into thousands of pieces of vexed passion
Simplicity of familiarity becomes complex restraint
When we make love,
The phrase loses all clarity

TASTE HER

May I long lick you?
Pressing my tongue flat against the base of your woman lips
Put your hands on my head,
Pulling my mouth into your deep trenches
Be selfish. Greedy
Open your legs wide,
Inviting my tongue inside you
Slow wine. Grind against my lips
Thrust your hips,
Allowing me to tongue-fuck your yoni
Wrap your legs around my neck
Feeling my tongue slip between your moist folds
Feel it sink into your silk-like wetness
Listen to your sloppiness,
How your stream trickles down between your ass cheeks
Feel your walls spasms... Shudder,
As I French kiss your entrance
Pause...
Nuzzle my head as I suck on you,
Causing your senses to dance
Taste your essential oils
It's purity. Unrefined. Organic
Concentrated goodness
Slide my tongue deep inside you,
Until you buck with involuntary convulsions
Unacceptable heated emotions

Audibly war sound of hard moans
Then suck on you with sudden and urgent want
So your voice explodes
Conveys surprise
Laces with disbelief
Compressed with sudden shock
May I suck on you, my love?

FULL

I want to fall between your thick thighs,
Filling them with the circumference of my gyrating waist,
Having you wrap your legs tightly around me,
A horny wife's embrace
Pressing against my body until they reach full capacity of me
I slide inside you,
Slow... deep... long
Your inviting walls clench and become obese with my girth,
Feeling me exceed the volume of your yoni,
Slowly crushing your fortification
Your natural bodily resistance crumbling
Grab hold of my back,
Pressing your hands against my muscles,
Digging your nails into my skin,
Your deep scratches becoming our communication,
As you take me in
Pull me into you... all of me
Feel your senses strain
Causing your mind and body to become overly extended
Filled with lust... with pleasures... with needs
I want you to feel your wetness thickens to fraught,
Weighted with the throbbing bulk of my hardness
Stretched ocean torrents
Overflowing with hard-pressed dissemination of my long thrusts
I want to fill you,

Fill your spasms until they become fat,
Plump with tingles
Have you clench...
Feel the fullness of your tightness become restricted
Overflowing the dimensions of me
I want to push in deep with my soulful, rhythmic strokes,
Fill you with the sounds of your own shudders as you gasp
Release obese moans
You expand with my girth,
Becoming inflated with overwhelming jolts of pleasure,
Until your yoni swells with nerve ending expansions
I want to fill you until...
Your orgasm bursts,
Full from the fullness of me

THE CYCLE

Gentle tongue motions ravishing your honey-coated lips
Music of pleasure is all I want you to perform, my love
Your body performing a chorus of rapturous applause
Territory of unreleased lust is where I wish for you to become lost
Constant tremors that cause you to flinch in your sleep,
My tongue aftershocks
This is how I want to please you,
Slide inside your consciousness with gentle, calculative tongue swirls,
Claiming your throbbing as my territory,
Procession of my passion evokes your praise
You wish to submit to my love,
To have me punish you,
Ravishing you until you surrender the joyful shudder of your release
Causing your bodily-quakes to proclaim the end of game...
Soft kisses...
Reset,
And start again

FINE WORK OF ART

My calloused fingertips,
Tracing the silhouettes of smooth, contrasting thighs
They navigate your rounded hips with familiar fascination
Inhalations whisper of longing
Our breaths catch,
While fingers orchestrate an exhaled symphony of moans
The flickering candle glow,
Dancing light and shadow across your golden, naked skin,
Revealing and concealing,
Adorning you with mystery,
Inflaming my desire within
I stare at your melanin wonders,
You are a fine work of art,
A masterpiece of Eros,
Passion's conquest
Sweat beaded like the tiniest of jewels,
Delicately balanced on your upper lip
Cheeks rouged by lust's inward furnace
Storm-tossed hair in damp disarray
Breasts rising and falling on subsiding breaths
Eyes heavy-lidded and drunken with love
Appetite now sated, your body lies spent,
Canopied by the lingering golden after glow
We were completely drunk with love,

We slowed down time,
Lingering long after the sun had slipped behind the hills
In the darkness, fireflies flashed out new constellations
We were lost in our own little universe,
Longing to never be found

TASTE

Her skin always tasted like my favourite things,
Sometimes like melted chocolate,
Sometimes like strawberries dipped in ice cream,
Sometimes like fine wine on a Friday night
I always knew just where to lick,
And she would drip,
Dripping honey
I had a sweet tooth,
And so for me, she would spread,
And like a bee, I would obey my Queen,
And trace my lips,
In search of her melanin wonders
The taste rushed to the chambers of my soul,
Pollinating the fields of wilted roses,
And breathed life into them as if for the first time
At that moment,
I knew that I had always known you,
And that tasting you,
That umami moment,
Where love, intimacy, compassion, sensual desire, and friendship all flood your pallet within the same knee-buckling epiphany,
Knowing that I might not ever taste anything again,
After tasting you just that one time

LOST

The moment I slide inside you is when I become lost,
Lost inside your wetness is where find my center
My peace,
Yet, my chaos
You navigate me with your rhythmic motions
Take me on a tour of pleasure each time you clench
Inform me of your historic paradise through your poetic nails etched into my skin
I am in a maze of sensations,
A labyrinth pleasures
Found…
No,
I wish to stay inside you… lost
Magic is what we create when we make love
Such chaotic magic is giving us both peace of mind
It is sensual love,
Built upon a foundation of mental intercourse
Our minds have indulged in cerebral foreplay
Intellect has been soft-sucked
We have tasted the juices of each other's thoughts
Desire has become the undertone of our dialogue
We crave… yearn for… lust for
To be lost inside each other…
Never to be found

EVERLASTING

I just want to...
No, I need to explore your constellation
Diving deep into your milky way
Finding a million reasons why you make every hair on my body stand
I want my lips to leave you breathless
Throat dry,
Thirsting for me to replenish it
I want to mark my territory in your mind,
Searching for that irrefutable connection,
My fingers dipping into your sea of passion
I want my arms wrapped around you,
Thoughts soliciting on the edges of your mind
Allowing you to guide me towards what my heart has been aching for,
A sensual journey into your world,
Filled with sinful desires, all matching mine
Let us explore, and try to find our fill
I am insatiable,
And my hunger for you will always remain a want, a need,
Forever starving for your lips
Kissing both until you shiver,
Kissing away every "I love you" you've ever regretted
I want to give you the ultimate pleasure,
When you yearn for my affection,
Body at full attention,

Slippery when wet is my only discretion
Face to face,
Our lips gently pressed
I want to explore all your body's continents
Queen, excuse my bold remarks,
But I just want to...
No, I need to...

FADED

Everyone tells me they love my work,
That my words make them wet,
Melt the ice cold chambers of their mundane sex lives
But then, when she says it...
I can't help but want to taste her pulse
Have the EDM rhythm of her want beating on my tongue
Dangerous levels of throbbing as I press my tongue gently against her nib,
Listening to her pulsation,
Conversing with her throbbing
Speaking in literal tongues
Feel the motion of her yoni's pounding heart
I long to have her coil her long, beautiful legs around my neck,
Scooping the fullness and tightness of her ass into my hands
Pull her towards me,
Kissing her clitoris
Gaze into the deep lust in her eyes
Seeing the desire in her soul
Taste her slow,
Slurp with long, lazy pulls
Envelop her rose bud with my lips
Suck fast... slow... fast... faster... pause
Her hands resting on my scalp,
Pulling my hair, caressing my head,
While I give her head

Have her pull my dome into her center
Open the horizons of her legs,
Inviting my tongue into its core
Heat of inflamed desire ready to ignite my tongue
Her fingertips glide across her yoni as I'm engulfing her jaws of fire
Creating static electricity
Kinetic frequency... generate vibrations
Reverberate inside her
Thunder booms through her walls
Jolts of pure pleasure strikes her body as I tongue-tickle her clitoris
I long to use my mouth,
Make love to her wetness,
Opening the flood gates of her orgasm
Her body spasms,
Causing her heart to fall between her legs
Her mouth wide open,
Creating beautiful, nonsensical grunts and wails
My mouth wide open,
Inviting the stream of her release,
And leaving her...
Faded

SHOW, NOT TELL

There are times... many times,
When I wish I could tell you,
Try to explain...how your sweet flavour,
Your rose-ebony-honey-yoni goodness makes my tongue sing,
A choir... soothing melodies
Causes it to yearn for your wetness
Want it to be glazed by your golden nectar
How it longs,
Often begs to caress your nib
Be able to long lick you,
To taste you
Stroke your clit with delicate motions
Sometimes, I wish I could tell you... explain
How your essence,
It becomes my essence
Evokes a dedicated purpose inside me
I am a follower of your yoni,
Of your woman paradise,
Of your ever-fertile, floral-ridden, honey-abundant garden between your highly flourished mountainous regions between your thighs
I praise your salty-sweet salvation,
Offering my taste buds redemption
You make my tongue's tambourine tingle,
Delicate chimes that ring in the roof of my mouth

Sometimes, I wish I could tell you... explain
How it feels while my tongue slides into your silk-like folds,
A relaxing bed of rose petals
How it feels when the waves of your woman ocean splash against my tongue,
Rippling over it,
Crest of your flesh rolling over it
How my tongue explores the deep trenches of your oceanic wonders
Become submerged... finds the soft shell
Discover your pink pearl... your most prized possession
Sometimes, I wish I could tell you... explain
How it feels when you release... when you cum
How your flowing river colours my mouth,
Decorates it with the artwork of your released pleasure
How my mouth becomes your canvas,
A gallery in which the exhibit of your climax is displayed
Sometimes, I wish I could tell you... explain
However, I rather show you

WORDS

I made love to her on paper,
Spilling ink-like passion across the sheets
I caressed her curves in every love letter,
Kissing up and down her thighs in short sentences and prose
I tasted all her innocence,
Without a spoken word,
Biting her lips, and pulling her hair in between the lines
I made her arch her back and scream,
And that was the beginning of our story,
Me writing poems inside of her with my fingers,
And ending with her soul on my lips
She was a true book of mysterious secrets,
Pressed between her pages like dried flowers
I ran my fingers along her spine,
Spreading her open,
Shaking her up,
Until they all came tumbling out
I read her thoroughly,
With keen attention to her sensual details,
Lingering at the climax of her story
I may have to read you again, my love,
For I fear I may have missed something

LANGUAGE

I love the way you grip my t-shirt when I slide into you
It's art
You create sculptures of cotton works,
Mould them into creative expressions of pleasure,
Convey the artistic imagination of my cock strokes
I love to stare into your eyes as our bodies become one,
Gazing into your soul,
I see colours,
The red of passion,
The aqua of tranquility,
The blue of openness,
The green of your organic delight
It's a kaleidoscope of tingles
I love the way your body speaks to me when you arch your back,
It is words,
Eloquent dialogue spasms,
Intelligent rhetoric shudders,
Philosophical wandering of pulses,
It is its own language,
An accent,
Prolific articulation of graceful profanity
I love the way you grab the bed sheets when my lips envelope your rosebud and gently pull it into bloom,
It is emotional,
Tornado rage,
Joyful delight,
Stunned surprise,

Dizzy confusion,
Pleading longing,
Demanding surrender
I love your bodily reactions when I fuck you...
It's how you communicate to me

BOOK 2

SOUL & SUSTENANCE

GROW UP

Foolish boy,
You've been inside of her for merely a few moments,
And you believe you've achieved something of note?
She's given you a few moments of pleasure,
And has distracted you from your vast emptiness,
But is that all you believe she could offer you?
You've ticked her off your growing list of conquest,
And she's given further rise to your toneless ego,
So you feel you've claimed her?
That you've ingrained yourself in her essence?
Boy, she has hidden treasures you know nothing of,
For you've failed to explore her heart,
Failed to satisfy her body, let alone her soul
Her mind awaits an intimacy far more naked than bare skin,
Her body awaits an intimacy so far reaching,
That it penetrates her main lands,
Where the rarest of birds sing divine melodies,
And the sweetest of fruits quenches any soul,
Rather than being garbage to her shorelines
Her body is an undiscovered human continent,
While her mind is a wild, tangled forest,
Vast and fertile,
With ancient temples and immense treasures concealed within,
Awaiting a more worthy of an adventurer

It's not your responsibility to regulate other persons' emotions,
Manage their insecurities,
Pacify their inner wars,
Heal their wounds,
And be the version of you in their minds
Understanding this,
You'll see how peaceful life becomes

I WRITE

I write for all you beautiful women,
With your struggles and scars,
With your silent sadness,
And unbirthed, faded dreams
I write for the weary-boned wonders,
The hearts wounded on love's battlefield,
Limping towards the sunset
I write for the crazy dreamers of love,
Never letting go of the idea that there is a love
out there awaiting them
I write for the survivors of heartbreaks,
The ones who gave their love to someone
unworthy of such cherished treasure
I write for all you beautiful women,
Hoping to open jaded eyes to rediscover their
hidden beauty that awaits
I am no magician,
But a Poet,
One who bleeds endless ink,
Hoping to give a life-saving love transfusion

Whatever you lose when you have decided to stand up
for yourself,
Protect your boundaries,
And begin to grow,
Were not meant to stay

Be confident, my love
Too many days are wasted comparing yourself to others,
And wishing to be something you aren't
Everyone has their own strengths and weaknesses,
And it is only when you accept everything you are,
And aren't,
Will you succeed...
Will you rise

MIRRORED LOVE

There lies a reflection in the mirror,
A mere perfected image of you
Smile
Tell her she's beautiful
Tell her you love her
Tell her you are proud of her and of how far she's come
Find strength through the confidence in knowing who you are,
And understanding nothing adds more value to you than understanding your worth
Understand that you are everything a man will desire and need,
As well as everything a boy will not understand, value, and take for granted
Love yourself first, my love,
Unless it won't mean anything coming from someone else

FOCUS

Do not allow yourself to lose focus,
For it's at this stage where it's easier to compare yourself to others
This, my love, is an energetic drain
Comparison with others robs you of the capacity to tap into your own innate abilities,
So that you may ge to live the life of your visions,
Not someone else's
Your power is that you are YOU,
You only lack the focus,
Not an issue of underachievement
Work on your self-focus,
And then you'll be bale to set the vison for your life,
YOUR rhythm,
YOUR journey,
And so you won't get distracted by events happening outside of your own lane

Your healing does not depend on someone else's apology,
For their lack of accountability is your confirmation to let go, and move on

Do it, my love
Be unorganized. Messy
That magical kind of mess that is its own kind of beautiful,
and one that no one but yourself will understand
Free yourself to roam the wonders of this life,
Wandering for the very sake of getting lost
You can't expect to find yourself,
To discover something new,
Before venturing out into the unknown
I may not know much,
But I do know this,
Freedom and love are found when we have the courage to let ourselves go

WONDER WOMBMAN

He never knew you were unstoppable,
That you were a Wonder Wombman,
That you have been blessed with a divine connection far greater than shallow minds can ever fathom
So, he tried to enslave you,
To contain your greatness by delivering relentless fists of words
Tried to devour you with the darkness of his lies,
But you are a Wonder Wombman,
A bamboo to his hurricane,
Bending, but never breaking,
Always regaining your true form in the radiant glow of the sun
Your worth made its own light that devoured his shadows,
As your tsunami of strength lay waste to his binding control,
Rising above hiss darkness like the moon in all her fullness and glow
You are clothed in dignity and courage,
And with the glow of God's grace,
You remain unstoppable,
You are a Wonder Wombman

Forgiving yourself constantly and generously,
So frequently that it becomes a habit,
Is a great form of healing most of what you punish yourself for,
Is wasted potential that exists in an abstract and invisible place only you can see

Expressing your needs,
Your emotions,
Your boundaries,
And your concerns,
Will not drive away persons who are committed to being in your life
You wanting to be treated with respect,
Knowing your worth,
And acting accordingly is never asking for too much in any kind of safe or healthy connection

Do not be in the company of persons who merely tolerate you,
Accept you,
Or like you with some conditions and provisions attached
Be in the company of those who absolutely adore your face,
Delight in your weird quirks,
your eccentricities,
And your contradictions,
And treasure the very strange things that you you,
YOU

Most found her strange,
For words were her aphrodisiac rather than diamonds,
And she preferred beautifully strung words than the precious strings of gold around her neck
Most found her odd,
But I found her perfect
For her every movement was poetry in motion,
Spoken words out of God Himself
She is the kind of beauty that falls gently on the lips,
But you may not notice it right away,
For hers is the essence that whispers ever so subtly to the mind, the body, and the soul,
Capturing all three,
Before entrancing your eyes

MEMORIES

I found some of the letters you had written to me,
Letters that I had tucked safely away from sight,
But not from memory
Letters laced with epigrams taken from our favourite songs
Are you being torn apart now that I ain't yours?
Do you still wonder who's gonna kiss me now that you're gone?
Is it killing you now that we are over?
As I gaze upon these letters,
Do I burn them?
I've lost all sense of time,
And I just wonder if you have too,
Or do I still linger in the deepest parts of your suppressed thoughts,
While you wander aimlessly on the shores of mine
"Every pain is bearable"
Is it?
Someone clearly hasn't been in the torture chambers of my heart,
Where I rigorously trod,
Trying to navigate an escape,
An escape from these memories

JUST MAYBE...

Maybe you're not broken,
For you are a warrior who has been slowly rebuilding yourself,
Regenerating and finding new ways of strengthening yourself
Consider that maybe,
Just maybe,
You need to be exactly where you are now,
For this moment can be the opportunity of a lifetime to embody who you've always been,
For it's better to have a warrior in the garden,
Than a gardener in the war
Just maybe...

You're responsible for your own growth and development,
So do not wait on others to forgive you or validate you,
Or hold yourself to an impossible standard to prove that you're a better person
It's simple, really,
You only need to decide that YOU ARE,
And back it up with your actions,
For what truly makes one a good person,
Is the fact that one cares about being one,
Rather than waiting on others to tell them they are

BE STILL

The caterpillar knows that the most impactful progress you will make in your life happens in stillness,
In the emptiness of it all
It may feel empty and dark,
But trust that there is a rich essence moving with you,
For progress isn't always obvious and palpable
It can exist in stillness,
Just as there is growth within decay,
And love within grief,
Surrender yourself to he unknown and unknowable,
And use your patience to make space for the emergence of that newness moving within
Turn the fullness within your emptiness into a message,
That you can make something out of this metamorphosis
Dig deep, trust more, and emerge being more than before,
For something epic always comes in the spring after a long, rigid winter

BLACK OR WHITE

Don't be ashamed of being "too quiet",
For there's always someone who will need your quiet and listening ear
Don't be ashamed of being "too clingy",
For there are always others who will need your openly affectionate love
Don't be ashamed for being "too weird",
For there are others who admire your will to stand out from the crowd
Don't be ashamed for being "too sensitive",
For there are others who respect and appreciate your connection to your inner feelings
What's a negative trait in one's eyes might be exactly what someone else is looking for,
It's never black or white

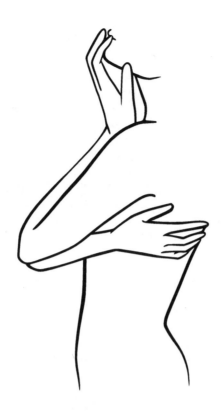

You will make mistakes,
You will act irrationally,
You will commit some wrong things that cannot be fully explained
Persons will dislike you,
And misunderstand you,
For their own reasons
However, none of these things make you a bad person
What may make you a bad person is if you refuse to try your best,
Be kind,
Learn,
And to grow

It's better to refrain from deep introspection,
And simply allow yourself to just be
Look at your mistakes,
Avoid self-flagellation,
Sigh and learn what you can and move on

Allow yourself to be human,
For there are going to be days when self-care means
allowing yourself to be angry,
Annoyed,
And even isolate from everyone
Embrace these moments,
For they are natural,
And apart of your humanly growth

Contrary to societal standards,
You are allowed to be a mess right now
You don't need permission to not have it all together at this point in your life,
Or have your future figured out
Embrace the fact that life hits us all,
But it's important to give yourselves grace in the midst of it all,
For we deserve at least that

Do not tie your healing to the hope that someone will
apologize for the wrong they did you,
Or even acknowledge it,
Or even realize they did it
Some will never accept that they did you wrong,
So live with it

Embrace changes that are happening to you,
Accept them and loosen up,
And allow yourself to walk a new path,
Even if it's an uncomfortable journey
It's only heavy because you shouldn't even be carrying a burden,
Just reference the past,
Embrace the present,
And move on into the future

Healing also means to sit down,
Reflect,
And take a honest look into the role you played in your own current suffering

...For when a flower doesn't bloom,
You fix the environment in which it grows,
And not the flower

Lord,
Bless the woman who craves and shines in her alone time,
For though her feelings are deeper,
Her thoughts are even deeper
Her alone time allows her to figure out her mood,
Where her aura is at,
And how to take each step in life to ensure she will rise again

WILD HEART PT1

She wasn't looking for a boy,
She was looking for a man
A partner to help slay her fears,
One by one,
Planting a flower garden over their graves
She awaits a man not intimidated by her sexuality,
A man who's not afraid to explore her inner fantasies,
Dusting them off, and bringing them to reality
She is a wild visionary,
And an insecure man will only make her feel imprisoned
But a secure man,
He'll set her mind and body free,
Unlocking her soaring dreams without fear of being judged
Rise on your growing wings, my angel,
And take flight as the sky calls you to its embrace,
For Wild Hearts were never meant to be caged

OVER-GIVER

Be careful to not grow into an over-giver,
For maybe you care because, deep down, you wish someone would care for you in the same way,
You give because you wish someone would give onto you in the same way
For in your commitment to give,
You become the human who constantly betrays their own values for the promise of somone's love,
Somone who burns just to keep others warm
Without feeling guilty, selfish, or self-indulgent,
I beg this of you,
Please extend to yourself the same care and attention you give to others

Just because you did something wrong in the past,
Does not mean it makes you a hypocrite to advocate against it now
You simply grew
Don't allow persons to use your past to invalidate your current mindset

Not because persons are more comfortable with your past self,
Means you have to be stuck in a persona YOU are not comfortable with
Their happiness and comfort are not your responsibility
You should not be taking steps back in your growth,
Or relive what you have outgrown,
Just to keep connections alive

YOU

I know most couples won't want to hear this,
But can we normalize something?
Is it wrong for us to say to our partner, "I'm sorry, but I am not sure I have the emotional readiness to handle this situation in the manner you deserve. Could we discuss this at another time?"
No way you're a bad person for acknowledging when you cannot be there for someone,
Even if it's someone you care for
How can you readily give love to others,
When you struggle to give it to yourself?

My love,
How can you be absorbing the opinions of persons who have not lived the life that you want,
And aren't at the level you wish to be at?
Their beliefs and energy will only get you as far as they are, my love,
And that's nowhere

True love is,
Loving someone when they least deserve it,
For that is when they need it the most

HER PATH

And what of your heart, my love,
Withering in the uncared for vines of your past?
Dying by the relentless fists of a thousand heartbreaks,
Met with countless words of pain
Like a lost soul,
Obediently fulfilling your prescribed role,
Will you continue to wander the never-ending maze of life's uncertainties?
Of past failures of love?
Oh, what a calamity,
Should your pawn of a heart never grow into the majestic queen you were meant to be
What misery,
Should you remain deaf to the whisper of your inner woman,
Pleading for you to smile at the person in the mirror,
Realizing a soul spark still lives within your weary bones,
Patiently awaiting discovery through careful archaeology
Woman,
I wish for you to sever the puppet strings which bind your heart to your past,
Dance no more to the noise of past boys,
Take a step as you move ahead to the grand adventure awaiting you,
Discovering the path God had lay before you
With each step,

The way will unfold,
With inner courage and vigilance,
Walk through you days, my love,
And allow no one to turn you aside

Shift your focus to your own shit,
For studying other persons' lives took for too much time
from your own
That's when you'll begin to thrive,
For minding your own business,
Is the most boss-up move you'll ever need to make

Do not worry if others,
Even close to you,
Do not understand your calling
It wasn't a conference call

WILD HEART PT 2

You see yourself as being "broken"
You look at the scars left from the many heartbreaks of your past,
And you believe you have no worth
You look down rather than up,
Believing you have something to be ashamed of
My queen,
Do not surrender to their smallness,
Do not be imprisoned by their earthbound ways,
For you have been blessed with having a divine connection much greater than your own understanding,
Clear your heart of all the anger and frustration left by the wrong presence of your past,
Erase their presence and soar beyond the fathoms of what your mind and body can ever imagine
Rise on the winds of freedom as you sail the blue oceans above,
Being majestic in the presence of the sun
Your very nature is to soar, my love,
So fly high and free,
For Wild Hearts were never meant to be caged

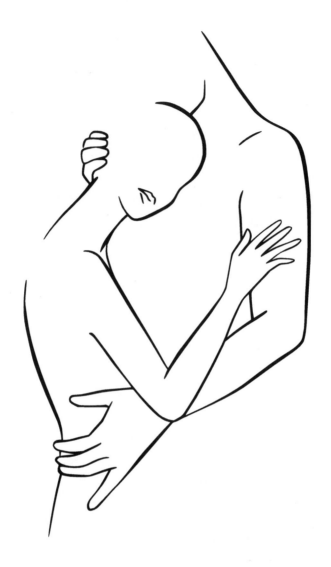

You are worth whatever magical
chaos you bring to the table,
And you know it,
So own it

You don't always need a plan
Sometimes,
You just need to breathe,
Trust,
Let go,
And see what happens

How to start healing?
Admit that you are unhappy,
Admit the reason, even if it's your fault
Admit you need to let go
Take a moment,
Breathe,
Then the healing will begin

How long will you continue doing what you are comfortable doing,
By putting off what you are capable of doing,
Simply because it makes you uncomfortable?

POETIC WOMAN

I wrote words on a picture you have of me,
And called it a poem for you;
Would you keep it?
Would you hold it as you drift into the realm of dreams?
And would you fumble for it in the morning as your eyes are still blurry with sleep?
I wrote words on the misted window in your bathroom,
And called it a poem for you;
Would you allow it to wash away your uncertainties?
Would it make you realize that your very smile controls the mechanics of my every heartbeat?
What if I were to hold you in my arms,
And allow my syllables to trace down your spine,
Illuminating your skin lie glow trails on highways seen from airplanes at night?
Would you finally take solace in knowing that you are most cherished?
What if you saw me writing;
Would you ask what if I'm writing a poem for you?
Would you cry when I tell you there's no need for that,
For your every presence is poetry in my life,
And our very love is God's poetry in motion?

EGO SO FRAGILE

Men, are we this weak?
Why are we taking advantage of nature's most valued creation?
The woman
We can't control our savage impatience,
So we make them the victims of our rabid temptations
From the days of the sacred woman,
Her mind, her body, and soul integration,
To now being treated as the recycling bins of our precious nation
Women, we owe you your rightful place at the throne
We as men are so weak… an ego so fragile
On behalf of us all, I apologize for taking you for granted
We lie, we cheat, steal, rape, and yet you still put up with us
To stabilize, adjust, and offer support for our disgusting habits
Men, why are derogatory names used to identify our women's social status?
Can't you see that they are our rock… the blood of our nation?
Together, women can single-handedly lead the masses
Our ego is so weak… so fragile
We are simply terrified of a black woman's magic… her strength,

That we are afraid to give her that opportunity to have a voice
We as men are responsible for the damage
We have failed to be strong, Failed to be protectors, Failed to be leaders Men, we have to fix this We call you too emotional, yet we are the ones who are overly sensitive, And we dare to associate inferiority with being feminine? How can we call the builders of a nation weak? Women keep us "leaders" grounded, But we try to rise above them, To loom down on them Cowards Are we that weak as men? Our masculinity that fragile? We as men are so fragile, but always the last admit it I thank you... the women of our nation, For continuing to be our rock... continuing to love us A love so infinite

Made in the USA
Columbia, SC
03 April 2025